" I like reading Sheri W
graphic nature. Her intir.
behavior keeps the stories active and engaging.  I'm a tough audience for film and literature because many authors lack knowledge to give depth to the psychology of the phenomena of which they speak or they make the story line incredulous, naive, or gapping. Wilson gives a real voice to the oppressed and silent victims. The writing helped me see the experience via the characters. It was empowering to see the connection between women across culture and race."

Tonya W. Lockwood, Psy.D., Clinical Psychologist, *Words of Life Center*


" The stories share the depth of women's experiences in unpredictable ways. These aren't typical sorrow to triumph stories – they turn and bend and twist in ways that reflect real human, real women's experiences. These stories left me in a thoughtful mood, with details remembered long after I read them. Wilson's stories are meaningful and touching, and reflect an artistic rendering of psychological truth."

Lisa Slade Martin, Ph.D., Clinical Psychologist, *Acclaim Academy, Philadelphia, Pennsylvania*

In Sheri Wilson's collection of short stories the landscapes shift between the urban, rural and suburban backgrounds of her diverse cast of heroines. Their stories drew me in with their intimate and sometimes lurid details. I picked up the book intending to read one story and read them all in one night. After the first story's twists and turns I wanted to see where the book would lead me. I felt taken inside these women's lives and honored with all the vivid, intimate and sometimes gritty details that you might not expect to find in a collection of everyday women's stories. One of the real treats was that these tales drifted unexpectedly between candid realism and surrealism. This book strikes a perfect balance of entertainment and enlightenment."

Nicole Cutts, Ph.D., *CEO Cutts Consulting, LLC and Founder, Vision Quest Retreats*


With a deep understanding of what drives human behavior, Dr. Sheri Wilson demonstrates why she is an author to watch in this decade and beyond. Dr. Wilson's collection of short stories examines the pathos, dignity, tragedy, and triumph that is 21$^{st}$ century womanhood. Presenting an ethnic and socioeconomic cross section of ladies, Wilson's writing gives us an up close and personal perspective of what drives her protagonists towards self-discovery and, ultimately, liberation. This is a must-read for those who want to see character come back to narrative fiction.

Spencer F. Johnson, M.D., Board Certified Psychiatrist and Independent Film Producer /CEO, *Skyrocket Productions, LLC and Reel Independent Film Extravaganza, LLC*

# Women Trapped and Free

A Collection of Short Stories

# Women Trapped and Free

## A Collection of Short Stories

SHERI A. WILSON

Women Trapped and Free. Copyright ©2012 Sheri A. Wilson. All rights reserved. Printed in the United States of America. No part of this book may be used or reproduced in any manner without written permission.

This book is a work of fiction. Names, characters, places, and events are imagined and any similarity to real persons or events is coincidental.

ISBN 978-0-9674381-1-5

For information regarding this book please contact:

Sheri A. Wilson
 C/O Seesaw Publishing
Seesawpublishing@yahoo.com

Cover Design by Peter Pfude, referred by Doreen Deterville

Author Photograph by Eupton C. Jackson


First Printing: October 2012

For Eupsher

# Contents

**A**GNES TULEY     1

**S**HEENA NOLAN     15

**I**SABELLA GOMEZ     29

**H**OLIDAY GIRL     42

**M**ARGARET "AMBER" OWENS     53

# Agnes Tuley

gnes Tuley loved to paint. Not the walls in her little clapboard house but prolific canvas paintings depicting human suffering. She painted whenever her hand or arm wasn't in a cast or when her fingers weren't broken. All of Agnes's broken bones happened at the cruel hands of Stumper, her live-in boyfriend of almost twenty years. Some of Agnes's family members wondered how it could be true. Agnes was an imposing woman with jet black skin who stood 5 feet 11 inches in her bare feet and weighed well over 250 pounds. How could she let a wisp of a man who barely stood 5 feet 7 inches and weighed 150 pounds on a good day give her the beatings of her life whenever he had an inkling to do so? That's how he got his nickname; he was literally a stump of a man compared to Agnes's enormous size. Stumper ruled the roost and he reigned supreme over Agnes. Her family wondered but said nothing and turned a blind eye to her broken bones and bruises. They concluded that if Agnes was allowing this sixty-year old drunken little man to beat her senseless whenever he pleased, he must be bringing home the bacon in the bedroom because they knew he wasn't bringing it home in cash. Besides, Agnes never complained and she steadfastly refused to leave him. Who were they to interfere? She was a grown woman, almost forty years old now.

Agnes and Stumper lived on the back roads of a little town called Castor, Louisiana, which had a population of just over two hundred people. The closest neighbor lived five miles away, so no one ever heard Agnes's screams when Stumper decided he wanted to have some fun and beat her, usually when he was drunk or about to get drunk. Agnes had never ventured out of Castor to the big city of New Orleans, had never enjoyed the Mardi Gras festivities or the night life that New Orleans had to offer. Even after New Orleans was on the road to recovery after Katrina and was a place of joy and celebration once again, Agnes stayed in Castor, leaving only when she needed to venture into the next little town to buy art supplies.

While Stumper was working an odd job, bedding one or more of the town whores or snoring in their bedroom after a day or night of heavy drinking, Agnes would drag her paintings outside and sit on the side of the dusty road where an occasional tourist would drive by, glance curiously at her paintings, then ask her how much she was selling them for. Agnes was desperate for money. Stumper's odd jobs paid next to nothing and most of his money was spent on booze and whores. Agnes always let the prospective buyer decide how much her paintings were worth. She couldn't afford to haggle, couldn't afford to hold out for the highest bidder. Sometimes her beautiful paintings sold for a mere ten dollars, other times they sold for a hundred dollars. In an occasional act of **self-preservation, Agnes** would sometimes hide the larger amounts of money in her tattered, dingy bra and give the smaller amounts to Stumper. Agnes spent the money she earned on art supplies.

It was an oppressively hot August afternoon in Castor when Agnes sat outside by the side of the road in her usual hunched over position, her mammoth legs spread as her enormous bottom straddled a cheap plastic chair which looked as if it would collapse beneath her weight but somehow never did. She wore a loose faded dress that looked more like a tent than a dress, her eyes squinting in the harsh sunlight. Surrounding her were five large canvas paintings depicting body shapes of women, their faces contorted in anguish, their toothless mouths gaping open, their bodies gruesomely bent like pretzels, twisted in agony. It was very quiet by the side of the road today, no tourists driving their jeeps or trucks or cars, no one at all. Agnes sat still in the stifling heat for two hours, her mind frighteningly unoccupied with not one thought. Suddenly she saw a red convertible of some sort chugging towards her in a cloud of dust as it made its way up the road. She squinted and stood up, using her hand to shield her eyes from the sun so she could get a better look at the approaching car.

A blonde woman turned off her engine and smiled at Agnes from behind the wheel of the car. She was wearing a halter top, shorts, and huge sunglasses. To Agnes, the woman looked very young, about twenty or so. The woman looked pleasant yet restless, as if she were searching for something she had yet to find.

"Hi ya!" the woman said cheerfully. "How far am I from New Orleans?"

Agnes shrugged. "'Bout two hours, I reckon," she grunted.

The woman frowned and then smiled again. "Damn it, I'm always getting lost." She glanced at Agnes's paintings. "Those are fab!" she exclaimed as she got out of her car to get a better look. "Wow! Did you paint these?"

Agnes nodded and grunted again. The woman looked curiously at Agnes.

"Not much for words, huh?" she said. "Well, that's okay. My friends say I talk way too much anyway." She proffered a slender hand, each long nail painted with a plethora of swirling colors. Agnes wiped her thick hand on her dress before she shook the woman's hand.

"I'm Christine. How much do you sell your paintings for?"

Agnes assumed her customary humble sales demeanor as she lowered her eyes. "Whatever you can give me will be fine, ma'am."

Christine looked at her incredulously. "What? No way! These paintings are awesome. I'll bet you could easily get a grand or two for each one, maybe more."

Agnes allowed her defeated mind to consider the possibility of earning that much money for only a second before she allowed herself a rare chuckle.

"Go 'head," she grunted. "Ain't nobody gonna give me that much money."

Christine took off her sunglasses, revealing clear blue eyes. Her eyes exuded the confidence of a young person who thought every possibility would automatically turn into reality.

"Yes they would!" Christine said excitedly. "Your attention to detail in the faces is unbelievable. Look at these women you paint, you can almost feel their suffering." She glanced around her for the first time. "Why are you selling your paintings out here on this dirt road? You'll never get any buyers this way." Suddenly Christine squealed with excitement. "I have the most fabulous idea! It's crazy but…"

She grinned at Agnes and then squealed again.

"Come take a drive with me to New Orleans! I'd love the company and you can sell your paintings in a big city totally full of life! My friends bailed on me at the last minute and I flew here from DC all alone. My friends totally suck." Christine gestured towards the convertible. "The GPS in this crappy rental sucks too. Can't believe I got lost but it's cool. So cool I met you, a real artist doing her thing."

Agnes glanced nervously at her rundown house. Stumper was inside, still sleeping off a night of boozing and whoring even though it was almost one o'clock in the afternoon.

"Come on," cajoled Christine as she lifted one of Agnes's paintings. The canvas was torn, but Agnes had dragged it out of the house anyway in hopes that it would still sell.

"What happened to this one?" asked Christine and then without waiting for an answer, she began to chatter about how heavy the paintings were as she struggled to load them one by one into the back seat of her convertible. Agnes remembered that Stumper had broken that particular painting over her head a few days ago for no good reason that she could remember.

Agnes watched helplessly as Christine loaded the final painting into the back seat of the car. "Oops, almost dropped that one," Christine giggled and then she rubbed her hands together and looked expectantly at Agnes.

"Let's go!" she chirped. "If we leave now, we can make it to New Orleans by three, right? You said it's about two hours away? What's the name of this town anyway?"

"Castor," Agnes mumbled. She stared at her paintings in the back of the red car.

"Yuck, sounds horrid," Christine said, wrinkling her small nose. She jumped into the convertible and started the engine. For a moment, Agnes thought she was going to drive off with her paintings. The air was still as she and Christine gazed at each other.

"Well?" Christine stopped smiling. Her voice was suddenly harsh as she narrowed her eyes. "What's keeping you here anyway?"

In that moment, Agnes couldn't think of one single reason to sit by the side of the road for another second. She looked at her faded dress, her dark legs ashy from the dusty road, and was suddenly aware of the suffocating silence all around her. No one was coming today, she thought, no one at all except this girl Christine.

The urge to escape in the red convertible suddenly took over Agnes's every thought, the impulse so out of character for her that even years later, she would be unable to explain why she did it. Without a word, Agnes squeezed her bulk into the front passenger seat of the small car. Christine squealed with delight again when she realized that Agnes was coming with her. She sped off as if she was afraid Agnes would change her mind, the tires of the car leaving a cloud of dust behind them.

Christine asked Agnes her name, then for the next hour Agnes listened in silence as Christine began to talk nonstop. She was born in California and relocated to DC with her parents at the age of five when her father got a government job in the Department of Labor. She dreamed of climbing in the Swiss Alps when she turned twenty-one in a few months but didn't have the money to travel to Switzerland and had no climbing experience. Christine's dad had been a professional surfer in California but after an ankle injury prematurely ended his career, he moved his family to DC, became a depressed government guy, gained weight, and basically stopped talking to Christine and her mother. Her mother was a self-employed artist who liked to take Xanax and paint pictures of floral arrangements.

"That's why I think what you do is so cool," Christine shouted over the sound of the engine as they sped down the open country road. "You're an artist. You create beauty, just like my mom. It wasn't his fault but my dad gave up on his art, his surfing. I've never forgiven him for that. I know he's depressed but geez, get over it, dude. That's what I always say."

Agnes wanted to tell Christine that getting over life's disappointments was easier said than done but she remained silent as the wind whipped across her stoic face. She was grateful that Christine was a talker, that she wasn't expected to say anything. Her mind was too dull and tired.

Christine must have finally grown weary of talking because she too fell silent as the GPS continued to instruct them to turn left here and to make a right turn there. They entered a little town complete with barely paved roads, a few county stores, a luncheonette, and one gas station.

"Have you ever been here before?" Christine broke the silence.

Agnes nodded. "I bought art supplies from the general store once or twice." She pointed to a big building on the corner that was in desperate need of repair.

Christine's face broke into a huge smile, almost as if she had momentarily forgotten that Agnes was an artist and they were on their way to New Orleans so she could sell her paintings.

"Cool!" Christine exclaimed as she parked in front of the general store. "Let's go in there. I'm getting hungry, maybe we can pick up some snacks for the road."

Christine climbed lithely from the car and bounded into the general store, Agnes ambling clumsily behind. Christine stopped in the entryway and looked around, then screamed in delight as she pointed to a sign in the back of the store.

"Oh my God! They do tattoos here! I just have to get a tattoo!" She tugged on Agnes's arm.

"You should get one too. How cool would that be?" Christine ran towards the tattoo sign with the eagerness of a puppy, Agnes trailing cautiously behind. She wondered if Stumper was awake and what he would think when he stumbled outside in the blinding brightness of the day and discovered that she and her paintings were gone. She could picture him standing by the side of the road, rubbing his red bleary eyes which would blink at the contrast between the darkened house from which he had emerged and the bright sun, scratching his small belly beneath his faded white undershirt and bellowing her name with the ferocity of a man twice his size.

A young guy with scraggly hair and two missing front teeth stared at Christine's breasts, then he grinned at her and asked her what kind of tattoo she wanted.

"Something wild, something absolutely wild!" Christine said. She looked at Agnes. "What should I get, Agnes?" she asked. "What kind of tattoo should I get?"

Agnes thought for a moment.

"A sparrow," she mumbled. Her mama used to always hum the song 'His Eye is on the Sparrow' when she was making Sunday dinner.

The guy started to clean his tattoo gun. "A sparrow," he snickered. "That's a real walk on the wild side."

For a moment Christine looked blank and then she let out a hoop of excitement as she hugged a startled Agnes. "That's cool! I so get it! An innocent sparrow ultimately demonized by the tragedies of life. A sparrow with red devil eyes and yellow fangs. Agnes, that's totally brilliant!"

Christine looked at the tattoo guy, her blue eyes sparkling. "A tattoo of a sparrow on my shoulder with yellow fangs and red eyes. Can you do it?"

"You got it," the guy mumbled as he bent over Christine's shoulder and went to work. Between winces and ouches, Christine asked Agnes, "Are you going to get a tattoo? You should go for it!"

"Naw," Agnes mumbled. She looked around the store. She was starting to get hungry. She reached into the pocket of her dress and pulled out a crumpled five dollar bill.

"I'll be back," Agnes grunted to Christine as she shuffled to the front of the store. As she walked away, Agnes heard Christine say to the tattoo guy, "She doesn't talk a whole lot but she's a brilliant artist. Can you believe I just met her about an hour ago? She was sitting on the side of the road all by herself in some town called Castor, trying to sell her paintings."

Agnes took a box of shortbread cookies to the register. A skinny old woman with frizzy brown hair and dull eyes was sitting behind the register staring lazily out of a small dirty window. The woman took the five dollar bill from Agnes and gave her fifty cents change.

"Enjoy them cookies, hon," the woman said in a voice that was raspy from smoking too many cigarettes. She stared out the window again.

Agnes opened the pack of cookies as she headed to the back of the store where Christine was getting her tattoo. As she approached, the tattoo guy barely even glanced at her. Agnes was used to being invisible to men but it hadn't always been that way. When she was thirteen her mama's brother, her uncle Leonard, started messing with her. He used to pinch her pubescent breasts when her mama and daddy weren't looking. Uncle Leonard frequently spent the night at her house after an evening of drinking and card playing with her daddy. At night when the house was still and everyone was asleep, he would sneak into the bedroom she shared with her eight year old sister Ruby and lie on top of her. He would breathe whiskey fumes in her face as he told her how beautiful she was, his large hands eagerly exploring her skinny body. His thrusts were slow and gentle at first and then became rough before he let out a yelp that he stifled in her pillow. After these encounters, he never lingered in her room and would creep away in the quiet of the house without a word, back to the sofa in the living room where he slept. When Agnes became pregnant a few months after the encounters with Uncle Leonard began, her sister Ruby told her mama about Uncle Leonard's late night visits to their bedroom. Agnes was surprised because she always thought Ruby was sleeping when Uncle Leonard was in her bed. Agnes's mama slapped and cussed Uncle Leonard and told him to never touch Agnes again. A few days later, her mama took Agnes to a dilapidated shack where a weird old lady who called herself Madam performed illegal abortions.

"You need to forgive your uncle Leonard, baby," her mama said on their way to Madam's house. "He may be a grown man but he's slow. Always has been, always will be. He don't mean no harm. Heck, Ruby's smarter than he is. We can't tell your daddy what Leonard did, baby. Your daddy would kill him. He would really kill him dead, then your daddy will go to jail. This will be our secret, okay? Don't you go tellin' your daddy about any of this nonsense with your Uncle Leonard."

After the abortion, Agnes cramped and bled for two weeks, wanting only to sleep. After the pain subsided and the bleeding stopped, she found solace in food. She ate until she was huge, until boys and men stopped looking at her. If she was fat, there would be no more men like Uncle Leonard doing nasty things to her in the still of the night, no more excruciating abortions, no more blood. The abortion must have ruined her insides because after she met Stumper she never got pregnant again. Stumper and Uncle Leonard were the only men she had ever had sex with.

Christine smiled as Agnes approached. "Well!" she said, pointing to the fresh tattoo on her shoulder. "What do you think?"

Agnes thought the tattoo looked more like a deranged bat than a sparrow. "It's fine," she said. Christine reached towards Agnes and took a cookie.

"Yum," she said, crunching loudly. She smiled at the tattoo guy who was picking his teeth with a jagged fingernail.

"Thanks for the tattoo, Mike," Christine said. She reached for a second cookie and stood up. "Can we share your cookies, Agnes? I just spent a lot of money for the tattoo. We can grab some real food in New Orleans."

They left the general store and climbed in the car. For the first time, Agnes saw the logo of a horse on the dashboard of the car. She quickly touched it with her finger. Christine noticed and smiled at her as she revved up the engine.

"I love Mustangs, don't you?" Christine mused as they drove. "They're so free to explore, unchained and unconfined. I wish I was a mustang."

"Me too," Agnes mumbled.

"You could be, you know," Christine laughed. "Your art can set you free. You can move to New Orleans and paint, drink wine, and make love. How cool is that?"

"Don't drink," Agnes mumbled again. She looked at the open stretch of road ahead. Christine glanced at her.

"So what's your story, Agnes?" she asked. "Why do you stay in Castor anyway? Are you married? Do you have kids?"

Agnes squirmed uncomfortably. She hated talking about herself. She was ashamed of her life and had nothing remarkable to say about it. Her life felt pointless like she was merely existing, waiting to die.

"No kids," she muttered, her eyes hooded. The memory of Uncle Leonard and the bloody abortion flashed through her mind. "Got a man, though."

Christine smiled. "Wow. Is he a hottie?" she asked. "Do you love him?"

Agnes stared straight ahead as she shifted in her seat, her eyes focused on nothing. "Don't know 'bout love. Been with him for a long time."

Christine's voice suddenly sounded somber. "Is he nice to you?"

Agnes was silent for what seemed like an eternity but in actuality she only paused for a few seconds.

"He beats me," she said with finality. "He been beating me for years now. Don't remember a time when he didn't lay his hands on me."

Christine took her eyes off the road as she stared at Agnes open-mouthed. The shock on her face made her seem younger than her almost twenty-one years, gave her a look of innocent indignation.

"Oh my God!" she yelled. "No way, Agnes! No fucking way! Kick his ass to the curb. Move to New Orleans, move anywhere. You can't go back to that guy!" Christine quickly swerved to avoid hitting a squirrel that was running across the road.

Agnes was startled at Christine's sudden outburst. In Castor, people were slow moving and unemotional. Even when Stumper was beating her, he did it with a kind of methodical calmness, even when he was drunk.

"Ain't no big deal," Agnes mumbled her lie, feeling as though she should be comforting Christine. "He just a lil' bitty old man. He don't really hurt me."

Christine's face was crimson. "It's just so…so not right," she fumed. "You seem like a really great person with an awesome talent and yet some jerk is knocking you around? I hate that shit. I really hate it, man." Christine lifted her chin with resolve as she sped down the road, both hands clutching the steering wheel. Agnes noticed Christine's blue veins through the whiteness of her skin.

"I can't wait until we get to New Orleans. You can start a whole new life with your art. This is your lucky day, Agnes. Man, this is too cool. Majorly exciting day for you." Christine pointed to a sign and grinned.

"Look, we're only thirty minutes from New Orleans!"

Agnes jumped as the car was suddenly filled with the raucous sounds of heavy metal music. Christine grinned sheepishly as she groped in her pocket and pulled out her cell phone."

"Sorry," she said apologetically. "I keep the volume up full blast on this thing." Christine held the phone to her ear.

"Hey Mom, what's up?" she shouted above the sound of the wind whipping through the convertible.

Agnes looked at the passing trees which they seemed to leave behind in a flurry of wind and dust. Maybe this little girl Christine was right, she thought. Maybe she would start over in New Orleans, somewhere, anywhere away from that shack and the dirt road. Stumper always said she needed him, that she was too fat and lazy to take care of herself but wasn't she already taking care of not only herself but of him, too? She couldn't remember the last time Stumper had even made any real money…

"You're lying!" Christine's blood curdling scream interrupted Agnes's thoughts as she jumped a second time. Christine was pounding on the steering wheel with her fists as the car zigzagged haphazardly across the road, tears streaming down her face. Agnes held onto her seat as she gave Christine a confused stare.

"Mom, it can't be true, it just can't be true…" Christine's scream had turned to a plaintive little wail as she clumsily pulled onto the shoulder of the road and turned off the engine. She fumbled to hang up the phone as her head sank onto the steering wheel, her shoulders heaving with sobs. Agnes was unsure of what to do as she watched Christine cry, then she clumsily put a broad hand on Christine's narrow shoulder, the shoulder with the fresh sparrow tattoo.

Christine cried for what seemed like an eternity and then she lifted her head. She stared into space, her eyes bloodshot with both shed and unshed tears. Her voice was clear except for an occasional quaver.

"It's my dad. He tried to kill himself. He's on life support and the doctors don't think he's going to make it. I can't believe he did it.

He's been depressed for a long time but I can't believe he actually tried to off himself."

Agnes's shoulders drooped as she cleared her throat. Her thoughts abruptly shifted from a new life in New Orleans to Stumper. She wondered if he was awake now and ready for his dinner.

"Guess you better take me back to Castor now so you can go be with your people," Agnes mumbled. "I'm real sorry about your daddy."

Christine shook her head and wiped her eyes with the back of her hand.

"No, I made you a promise," she said stubbornly as she gulped. "I'll drop you off in New Orleans and then I'm going to the airport to fly back to DC." Christine suddenly grasped Agnes's hands and held them tightly; her blue eyes wide and filled with the desperation of a young person fighting to hold on to her innocence.

"Promise me you won't end up like my dad with broken dreams. Promise me you'll make your dream of becoming an artist come true. Okay?"

Agnes looked away from Christine's young face, still amazingly hopeful despite the news she had just received about her father. Agnes nodded dully as the grim reality of her life struck her like a sword.

"Yeah, I promise," she grunted as she reached for the door, still looking away from Christine. "I gotta use the bathroom. Gonna use the woods."

Christine nodded bravely as she wiped away a fresh set of tears.

"I'll wait for you right here."

Agnes climbed laboriously from the small car and lumbered into the woods. She ignored the sweat that poured down her forehead and stung her eyes as she started to run. She ran until she couldn't hear Christine calling her name over and over again in a voice that was becoming increasingly frantic, until she couldn't hear Christine's rapid little footsteps tentatively pursuing her through the woods, until she couldn't hear the sounds of Christine's footsteps retreating back to the road, until she couldn't hear the roar of the little convertible as Christine finally gave up and drove away.

Two days later on a hot August morning in Castor, Louisiana, Stumper gave Agnes a black eye and threw a steaming pot of oatmeal on her that she had prepared because he forgot to tell her in his drunken haze that he wanted grits and eggs for breakfast. As she lay motionless on the floor of her rundown little kitchen with her eye throbbing and her skin burning, she vaguely wondered what had happened to her paintings that she had left in the back of the little red convertible.

# Sheena Nolan

It was a Saturday afternoon and the playground was filled with the raucous sounds of children playing, their hearts free, concerned only with the next adventure on which they planned to embark in the fenced-in play area in which childlike imagination had no limits. Sheena Nolan squinted in the warm September sun as she watched her five-year old daughter Samantha run from the sliding board to the seesaw smiling, laughing jubilantly, without a care in the world. Sheena sat silently on a wooden bench as she watched her only child with an eagle eye, afraid of unseen demons that might lurk unnoticed on the playground. Someone coughed and Sheena pulled her eyes away from her daughter for a moment, turning briefly toward the sound. The cough sounded bronchial and Sheena winced slightly. Another fear was the numerous germs that Samantha brought home seemingly every day from kindergarten. Before Samantha was born, Sheena barely noticed coughing or anyone's illnesses for that matter, her immune system boosted by the vitamin C supplements she took daily. Now no amount of vitamins seemed to protect her from the ruthless germs that seemed to ravage Samantha's school. Whenever Samantha was ill, Sheena became sick within a few days and vice-versa. A petite blonde woman sitting on the bench smiled at Sheena as she coughed again. Sheena forced a smile as she ran her hands through her chestnut hair which fell in thick waves to her shoulders. She hadn't noticed the woman before and wondered how long she'd been sitting there.

"These kids," the blonde woman sighed and smiled again. She had creases around her eyes, the universal sign of a tired middle-aged woman simultaneously juggling the aging process, work, and motherhood. "I stay sick all the time," the woman continued. "Dylan and Josh just got over a cold and were generous enough to share it with me. I must remember to thank them for their generosity."

Sheena vaguely recalled Samantha mentioning two boys named Dylan and Josh. Sheena thought Samantha had told her they were bullies.

"Dylan and Josh are my twins," the woman said, pointing at two brown-haired boys who were shouting in glee as they wrestled a football from a third boy. She shifted the sunglasses perched on top of her head. "Which one is yours?"

Sheena pointed to Samantha, who had abandoned both the sliding board and seesaw and was now part of a group of kids hovering over some kind of hand held computer game being played by a chubby red-haired boy with a plethora of freckles. The woman looked at Sheena and smiled broadly as she extended her hand, revealing fingernails bitten down to the nub.

"I'm Carolyn," she said brightly, her blue eyes weary. Sheena hesitated for a second, wondering if Carolyn had coughed into the outstretched hand, then she quickly shook her hand. "Sheena," she replied briefly, wondering if it would be rude to reach inside her purse and retrieve her hand sanitizer. Carolyn saved her the trouble by standing up abruptly.

"Excuse me, must intervene," she called cheerfully over her shoulder to Sheena as she walked toward her twins who were now pounding the third boy in the head with the football. Sheena reached inside her purse and squirted a generous amount of orange citrus sanitizer into her hands. She welcomed the cool feel of the liquid on the hot summer day. As she rubbed her hands together, she noticed a tall black man with very long dreadlocks pulled back into a ponytail and two children, a girl and a boy, striding briskly toward the playground. That was typical of the racial make-up in Silver Spring, Maryland; nothing stayed racially homogenous for too long. Her thoughts shifted to her husband Paul. Vaguely, she wondered how he was doing. They had met seven years ago at a fundraiser. Paul was a senior vice-president and general manager of a retail marketing firm and was traveling on business as usual, which for the past three years he did every weekend, twelve months a year. Sheena had always found it ironic that Paul became increasingly absent when Samantha hit the terrible twos. Samantha adored her father. His absences gave him deity status in her five-year old mind, something that Sheena hated to admit bugged her to no end. She wondered when she would be held in such high regard, the one who juggled a forty-hour work week as a guidance counselor in a middle school while keeping up with homework and the overall happenings in Samantha's kindergarten class while shuttling her back and forth between swim lessons, girl scouts, and piano lessons. She recalls laughing wryly but saying nothing when Paul had asked her if she thought they should have another baby. She was exhausted at thirty-nine years old, felt more like fifty. It made her both angry and sad that Paul was so out of touch with her weariness he actually believed she could handle another child, much less an infant.

Carolyn returned to the bench with a deep sigh and shook her head. She then turned her bright smile to the black man who had approached the bench and was sitting down.

"Boys!" Carolyn exclaimed as she tossed her hair, looking at him with a wide grin. "What will we do with you all?"

Sheena blushed as she glanced at the black man, who flinched as if he had been slapped. She had dated a few black men in college and knew that hearing a white person refer to them as boys might make for an angry moment. Oblivious to the unintentional racial undertone of her comment, Carolyn kept chattering away about her twins and the football. Her childlike oblivion made Sheena smile a little. The man seemed to relax when he noticed Sheena's smile. He looked down at his large brown hands, which were clasped in front of him. Sheena noticed he was trying to conceal a smirk which made her want to laugh.

"Well!" Carolyn exclaimed as she stood up and smoothed her Capri pants. "I guess I'll round up the troops and make a beeline for the minivan. It's hamburger helper tonight. No, maybe they want Sloppy

Joes or turkey for the Tryptophan. Whatever puts them to sleep the fastest." She laughed at her own joke as she slid her sunglasses from the top of her head to conceal her eyes. "Dylan, Josh, let's go!" she called. She gave Sheena a final sunny smile. "Nice to meet you," she chirped and then she was gone.

Sheena and the man sat silently for a moment as if relishing the sudden calm that enveloped them since Carolyn's nervous energy had made its grand exit. Sheena and the man glanced at each other at the same time. The man extended his hand.

"I'm J.T.," he said, his voice deep and steady, very sexy in a breathtaking sort of way. Sheena shook his proffered hand.

"Sheena," she responded, noticing that his hand was not only large but warm, emitting both strength and comfort. They were silent again as they watched the children playing.

He pointed to Samantha.

"Is that your little girl?" he asked. The sun accentuated his hazel eyes which were staring off into the distance. Sheena nodded and looked at the two children J.T. had brought to the playground.

"Your son and daughter," she stated rather than asking.

"Yep," he replied as he ran a hand through his dreadlocks.

"Miles is nine, Nyla is seven." J.T. gave a brief laugh that sounded almost like a bark. "They're pretty well-adjusted. My ex and I didn't fuck them up too badly." He stopped short and gave Sheena a sheepish look. "Sorry," he apologized. "I don't usually talk that way around ladies."

Sheena shrugged.

"It's fine," she said and then looked at him incredulously. "Why are you telling me all this?" she said, only half joking. "I don't even know you."

J.T. smiled as he stretched his long legs. His teeth were very straight and very white. Sheena couldn't help but wonder if they were veneers. "You do know me," he said. "My name is J.T. I have two children and an ex-wife."

Sheena laughed. "Okay, I'll play along," she said. Truthfully, she was enjoying this little game of getting-to-know-you. "Question number one. What does J. T. stand for?"

He chuckled. "Do you really want to know?" he said, his voice comically low and mysterious. "Do you think you can handle it?"

Sheena rolled her eyes in an exaggerated fashion. "I'll take my chances," she said.

J. T. used his hands to do a drum roll on his thighs, which Sheena noticed were well-muscled beneath his jeans.

"Jamison Tyler, Jr., but please don't call me that. Everyone calls me J.T. for short."

"I think Jamison is a nice name, but I will honor your request," Sheena replied in an exaggeratedly somber tone. Just then her cell phone rang.

"Excuse me," Sheena said hastily as she rummaged through her purse. She looked at her cell. It was Paul. "Excuse me," she said again, turning slightly away from J.T.

"Hello?" she said. Paul was still in New York and wouldn't be back Sunday night. She should expect him sometime on Monday instead. Paul asked how she and Samantha were doing and then said he had to take another call.

Sheena hung up and put her phone back into her purse.

"Good news or bad news?" J.T. asked quietly.

Sheena shrugged. "Neither," she said dismissively. Just then Samantha came running over. She leapt into Sheena's arms.

"Mommy, Jake has a Nintendo 3DS! Mommy, I want that too, can I have one?"

"What is that?" Sheena smiled at her daughter, feigning ignorance. J.T. laughed.

Samantha sighed impatiently as she pursed her lips and rubbed Sheena's face with her tiny hands. Her palms felt moist and sticky. "It's a really cool game mommy, can I have one?"

"It'll set you back about two fifty," J.T. muttered. Samantha looked at him for the first time. "What?" she whined. She glared at J.T.

"It's *may* I have one. Don't be rude," Sheena chastised her daughter. "We'll talk about it later."

"Okay," Samantha relented. She squirmed out of Sheena's arms and ran back to the playground.

J.T. laughed. "That little lady won't be speaking to me any time soon," he said. He gazed at Sheena. "She looks like you, did you know that?"

Sheena shrugged. "I guess so," she said. "She looks a lot like her father, too."

This time it was J.T.'s turn to shrug and then he looked at her so intensely she felt unsettled, vulnerably exposed in a way that was strangely arousing.

"Maybe, but she looks like you, too. His gaze remained steady. "Same cute round face, pretty skin, sparkling green eyes."

J.T.'s attention to her appearance was flattering. To Sheena, it seemed like Paul hadn't really looked at her since Samantha was born.

"Round face?" she pretended to be insulted. "Are you trying to say my face is fat?"

J.T.'s eyes left her face and perused her body. "Not fat, not thin, just right. Everything I see is just right."

Their eyes lingered on each other just a little too long. Sheena quickly looked away, wishing her phone would ring, wishing Samantha would come running over again, wishing the sky would fall down, anything to interrupt the uncomfortable intensity of this moment.

***

Sheena turned forty years old three weeks after meeting J. T. at the playground. Her birthday happened to fall on one of Paul's rare weekends in town. She was so exhausted after a busy day of work and caring for Samantha, she wanted only to fall into a deep uninterrupted slumber. However, Paul insisted on celebrating her birthday by taking her to dinner at an upscale restaurant in northwest DC. She knew Paul's motives were less than honorable; Sheena thought he was combating his own form of superficial guilt which stemmed from being away from home so often.

Sheena left Samantha in the care of her trusted babysitter, a 22-year old young woman named Maya who worked as a teacher's aid in Samantha's classroom during the week and moonlighted as a babysitter on the weekends to make ends meet. Maya was very pretty in a biracial sort of way and perky to a fault. Samantha adored her. Sheena suspected Paul liked her too. On more than one occasion, she had noticed him checking out Maya's equally perky backside.

***

Paul drove his black Mercedes S600 sedan to the valet parking at the restaurant and handed the valet his key. They walked inside the restaurant to their reserved table, Paul tersely glancing around his surroundings as he always did. He stepped back and pulled out Sheena's chair as she sat down. Paul hungrily studied his menu then smiled broadly at Sheena.

"Happy birthday, darling," he murmured. "Are you having a great time?" Sheena stared at Paul for a moment, wondering what made him tick.

"Great," she echoed hollowly. She studied the wine list. As usual, she knew she would be drinking alone. Paul told her he had sworn off alcohol after being diagnosed in college with genetically elevated liver enzymes.

Sheena rummaged in her purse for a compact. She and Paul were together so infrequently that when he was around, she liked to look her best. This was not particularly for him, but instead to prove to him that his absences didn't make her fall into an empty abyss, that she was still a beautiful and desirable woman. As a handsome black man with long dreadlocks approached their table, Sheena barely glanced at him as she peered into the mirror of her compact and retouched her lipstick.

"Good evening. My name is Jamison. Unfortunately I will not be your server tonight but will start you out until your server is available. Would you like to begin the evening with a cocktail?"

Sheena looked up abruptly and stared in shock at the man she had met at the playground three weeks earlier. J.T. smiled at her. It was a smile that to anyone would appear polite and perfunctory, but to Sheena she knew what was behind the smile. Her heart skipped a beat as she quickly snapped her compact shut, pinching her finger in the process. Paul didn't notice as he ordered a glass of water, but J.T. did.

"Is your finger okay, ma'am?" he asked in that same deep sexy voice she remembered from that day in the playground. He smiled at her again.

"Hmmm, what was that?" Paul murmured absent-mindedly, looking around the restaurant again.

"It's fine, thank you," Sheena replied, wondering what it would feel like to have J.T.'s lips on her pinched finger. She quickly pulled her gaze away from J.T. and blindly perused the wine list.

"Red wine, please," she said nervously.

J.T.'s mouth lifted slightly in one corner as he smiled at her.

"Yes, ma'am," he said and then he looked at Paul.

"I'll be right back with your drinks."

Sheena watched J.T. leave, then she stood up. She felt a sudden urge to get away from Paul for a moment, to escape and be alone with her thoughts. Truth be told, she was already alone. Except for small talk, Paul rarely had anything to say to her these days.

"I need to go to the restroom," she said. "I'll be back."

"Hmm, what's that? Oh, that's fine, darling," Paul said. He didn't look up as he read a text message on his cell phone.

Sheena left Paul at the table staring at his cell phone and headed toward the restroom self-consciously, wondering if J.T. was watching her. Tonight she was wearing a form fitting red dress, Paul's favorite color. She had gained weight since Samantha was born and was no longer the svelte size four she used to be. She was squeezing into a size eight these days, sometimes even a ten if she was shopping at an inexpensive clothing store. She thought her weight gain might be the reason Paul had started to keep his distance both in and out of the bedroom, probably because she was no longer the skinny woman he had fallen in love with seven years ago. Sheena remembered that when she dated black men in college, they seemed less concerned about a woman's weight than the white guys on campus. One black boyfriend had even urged her to gain weight, something that still amazed her to this day.

As Sheena placed her hand on the door to the restroom, she felt someone's lips graze her hair and then gentle large hands lifted her hair and kissed her neck. She didn't turn around as her knees almost buckled. She closed her eyes, wondering if she dreaming.

"Never thought I'd see you again," a deep voice whispered in her ear. She smelled peppermint on the breath. A black woman leaving the ladies room gave them a scathing look, which they barely noticed. J.T. grabbed Sheena by the hand with urgency and quickly led her down the hall to a small storage closet beside the kitchen of the restaurant where he closed the door and pushed her against the wall with the weight of his body. Sheena felt his body quiver as he kissed her tentatively as first and then deeper and deeper, their bodies so close it felt to both of them as if they were fused together. J.T. breathed in deeply as he lifted Sheena's dress and pulled at her panties. Sheena stroked his dreadlocks then moved her hands to his face, reveling in its dark satiny texture. She could feel the sweat from his face saturate her hands. She had a sudden urge to rub his sweat all over her face and then she remembered Paul, remembered where she was.

"Not here," she gasped breathlessly. "We can't, J.T. Not here."

J.T. buried his face in her hair.

"When? My shift is over. When can I see you?"

Sheena hastily reached into her purse and pulled out a pen and a scrap of paper. Quickly, J.T. grabbed the pen and paper from Sheena and scribbled his number on the paper.

"Call me, okay?" he whispered, pressing the paper into her hand. He gave her a final look of longing before he hastily retreated, leaving her standing alone in the storage closet.

Sheena's knees felt weak as she quickly scampered into the ladies room. She shoved the paper with J.T.'s number into her purse and looked in the mirror. Her hair was tousled and her make-up was smeared. She brushed her hair and reapplied her make-up with shaking hands. Sheena leaned on the vanity as she closed her eyes. She was grateful that J.T.'s shift had ended, that he was not going to be their server. She was so engrossed in her thoughts she didn't hear the door open.

"You'd better hurry back to your table. Your husband will wonder what happened to you."

Sheena jumped as she opened her eyes and looked in the mirror again. This time, she saw an old woman with stooped posture and a kind smile. The woman's eyes had a cloudy look that Sheena had seen before in the eyes of elderly people. The woman's silver hair was illuminated by the bright lights in the restroom.

"Oh!" Sheena gasped. "Sorry, you startled me."

"I know I did, my dear." The woman stood beside Sheena and gazed at her own reflection in the mirror. She sighed as she patted her hair.

"No matter how old I get, I still see a young woman when I look in the mirror. Of course I know it's not true, that I'm no longer young at all. It's very sad how quickly time passes for all of us no matter how young or old we are. What do you think about that, my dear?"

Sheena smiled. "That's true," she replied politely as she walked toward the door.

The woman placed a wrinkled hand on Sheena's arm. The hand was pale and spindly, covered with blue spider veins and moles.

"I saw you with the beautiful young man," the woman began.

Sheena stared wordlessly at the woman, her heart suddenly pounding so hard, she thought it would explode through her chest. Questions began to race through her mind. Who else had seen her, she wondered. Had Paul seen her too? Had the entire restaurant witnessed her infidelity? Would the dining room greet her with a dead silence when she returned to her table?

"Why, you look like you've seen a ghost. Don't worry, no one else saw you," the woman said as if reading her mind. She gave Sheena a reassuring smile.

"I won't keep you because I know you must return to your table and to your husband. However, the way you kissed the young man and the way he kissed you, I dare say you are married to the wrong man."

"I'm sorry," Sheena stuttered. "I didn't mean…"

"The woman kept her hand on Sheena's arm.

"I stayed with the wrong man for all the right reasons or so I thought," the woman continued as if Sheena hadn't spoken.

"I stayed for the sake of my children, because of finances, because of our shared home, because I didn't want to humiliate my husband with a divorce." The woman sighed as she stared deep into Sheena's eyes.

"Do you know what's so funny? When my husband died, I was seventy years old. My children finally told me they wished I had left the marriage because I wasn't happy with their father. They knew that

I wasn't happy all along. I was in love with another man in the next town, passionately in love, but I never acted on it. Somehow though, they knew. I wonder if my husband also knew. Do you love your husband, my dear? Do you want to live the rest of your life with him? Is he the man for you?"

The tears began to stream down Sheena's cheeks for what seemed like an eternity. Finally, she shook her head and looked down at the floor.

The woman gently dabbed at Sheena's tears with her bony fingers.

"The young man you were kissing so passionately may not be the love of your life but neither is your husband," she said. The woman then lifted Sheena's chin with a trembly hand. Her voice quavered with age, yet was filled with strength.

"Take my advice. Save yourself and find happiness. Do you have children?"

Sheena's voice was barely a whisper. "I have a daughter."

The woman nodded knowingly.

"If you don't have the strength to find true happiness for yourself, remember this. Your marriage is the blueprint for the relationship your daughter will ultimately have with a man. Teach her how to be happy, how to make the choices that will lead to personal fulfillment. Do not confuse personal fulfillment with selfishness. Lead through example, my dear."

The woman gave her arm a reassuring squeeze then smiled at her a final time before she quietly slipped out of the restroom.

***

Paul and Sheena returned home from the restaurant after a very quiet dinner. Paul grinned at Maya the sitter as he paid her while Sheena checked on Samantha. She was sound asleep in her pink little bed, breathing evenly. Her tiny face looked angelic even in the darkness.

"I want you to be happy, my darling," she whispered as she kissed her daughter's warm cheek. Sheena was stroking Samantha's face when

Paul walked into the bedroom. He briefly squeezed Sheena's shoulders.

"Nice evening we had, huh?" he murmured to Sheena as he stared at his sleeping daughter.

Sheena squared her shoulders as she took a deep breath and looked at her husband.

"Paul, we need to talk…" she began but Paul interrupted her.

"I know I'm not as attentive as I should be," he said calmly as he continued to stare at Samantha's sleeping form.

"I'm a lot like my dad. I take care of my family but I'm not much for all the lovey dovey stuff. Taking care of my family is more important than being mushy, even if it means I have to be away from home more than you would like me to be. The thing is, I love this little girl more than anything in the world. You have no idea how much I love her."

"I know Paul, but…" Sheena began again. Paul interrupted her a second time. This time he looked at her and smiled placidly.

"Forty is a funny age. Turning forty makes women do weird things. My mother went through the same thing."

Sheena stared at him in silence as he continued to speak.

"I can't be here with you all the time. You know how my job is with all the traveling and late night meetings. It's been that way for a long time and I don't see it changing any time soon. In life, we all have to make sacrifices. Life is not a fairy tale, Sheena."

He smiled at Samantha again and then looked at Sheena. His face was pale and insipid against the shadows in the darkened room as he spoke.

"If you divorce me, I'll take Samantha and I'll disappear. You'll never find me. You'll never see her again."

Sheena stood rigid from shock as Paul leaned over and kissed her on the cheek. His lips felt like stone.

"Good night, darling." Paul turned on his heel and left the room. Sheena heard him whistling softly as he walked into his home office and closed the door.

Sheena sat motionless by Samantha's bed for a long time, absorbing Paul's words. Finally, she stood up and walked into the kitchen where she had left her purse. She sat at the kitchen table and rested her head in her hands. She listened to the clock on the wall as it slowly ticked away, until her head slipped from her hands, until she fell asleep to its rhythm. Sheena smiled in her sleep as her dreams took her away to another place and time, to a world filled with warm tropical islands and exotic colorful plants, to a world where she, J.T., and Samantha held hands as they strolled the beach together every evening to greet the orange sunset overlooking the clear blue ocean.

It was almost 3:00 am when Sheena reluctantly awakened from her dreams in the dark kitchen, her arm red and cramped from the weight of her head resting on it for the last four hours, her back stiff from falling asleep in the kitchen chair. Sheena blinked before she slowly reached into her purse and gazed at the piece of paper with J.T.'s number on it. She rubbed the small piece of paper between her thumb and forefinger. Suddenly the dream seemed far away, cast back into a world which was never meant to exist for her. Her eyes were filled with tears as she pressed her lips against the paper. She held the paper against her lips until she finally pulled it away and tore it into what seemed like a hundred little pieces of her heart.

# Isabella Gomez

Manuel Gomez shook his head as he looked at the fresh red scratches on his wife's arms.

"That boy knows better, Isabella, I know he does," Manuel panted furiously as he zipped up his landscaping uniform. "I don't care what those doctors say. He knows what he's doing and he knows right from wrong. He has no respect for you because you treat him like a baby."

Manuel rolled up his sleeves, revealing hairy brown arms.

"Look at my arms. See, Isabella, no scratches. He attacks you because you allow it. Beat him, make him listen to you."

Isabella shook her head. "No beatings, Manuel. The doctors said that will make him worse, will make his autistic disease worse."

Manuel gave a contemptuous snort as he sat on the bed in their modest bedroom and put on his shoes. Isabella noticed that the bald spot on his crown was spreading.

"The doctors say this, the doctors say that. This is all I ever hear from you, Isabella. You are here with him all day. The doctors do not care because they are not the ones who are with him all day, all night. You must protect yourself. He will not always be a small boy of four forever. One day he will be a big man much taller than you, much bigger than you. Make him listen to you now, Isabella."

You are not here all day with him either, Isabella thought. Instead, she nodded in agreement because she wanted the conversation to end.

"I will try, Manuel. I will try it your way."

Manuel gave her a quick hug as he smiled, pleased.

"You will see that he will listen to you after you get tough," he said as he walked out of the bedroom. Isabella followed him to the kitchen where he grabbed his lunch that she had dutifully packed for him the night before. He poured himself a glass of orange juice, gulped it down and then headed to the front door of their two bedroom apartment.

"No breakfast this morning?" Isabella asked.

Manuel shook his head. "I will grab something from McDonald's."

McDonald's, Isabella said to herself. Sometimes Manuel spent money like they were rich. He kissed her on the cheek.

"You will see that my way with Carlos will also work for you. No more scratches, no more hitting you. You will see."

Manuel kissed her and opened the front door of their apartment.

"You have a good day, Isabella. Hang in there. Next year, Carlos can go to the special school and your days will be much easier."

Isabella watched Manuel as he trotted down the steps whistling, his bag lunch swinging from side to side. Disconsolately, she closed the door and then looked at the clock on the wall in their cramped living room. Hanging above the clock was a picture of Jesus, his hands clasped in prayer. It was 7:00 am. Her neighbor Maria would be dropping off her seven month old twin babies any minute now. Babysitting little Jose and Cristina didn't pay a lot of money but it was better than standing on her feet all day like Maria did cleaning houses for rude wealthy strangers or scrubbing filthy toilets in restaurant like her older sister Lena. Two seconds later, she heard a crash coming from Carlos's bedroom.

Isabella closed her eyes and touched the crucifix pendant around her neck as she said a quick prayer. Maria was starting to worry about Carlos's temper. She hadn't said anything yet but Isabella could see the look of apprehension in her eyes each morning when she left her babies with Isabella, worried that one day Carlos would hurt them. Isabella knew the only reason Maria continued to leave her children with her was because she couldn't afford another sitter, much less a real daycare center. Isabella wondered if life may have turned out differently had she and Manuel stayed in Mexico. Back home,

Isabella and Manuel had their parents and a huge extended family that would have helped with Carlos. There were a lot of Mexicans here in Texas but they weren't family. To Isabella, it seemed like everyone in America looked out only for themselves and Mexicans were no different. Manuel and her sister Lena had green cards but Isabella was in the country illegally. She didn't particularly care about her immigration status but Manuel desperately wanted to become a citizen like Carlos, who was born in Texas.

Isabella glanced at the leather belt that Manuel had left draped across their faded floral couch. She picked it up and threw it behind the couch. Isabella hated the way Manuel handled Carlos, hated witnessing the beatings he gave their son. She thought that his brand of discipline didn't improve Carlos's behavior as Manuel was convinced it did. He merely cowered when his father was around, refusing to speak the few words he knew.

Isabella caught a glimpse of herself in a small mirror that hung on the wall next to the clock and couldn't believe how much she had aged since leaving Mexico, marrying Manuel, and giving birth to Carlos. She had once been a beautiful petite Latina with big brown eyes and long luxurious black hair that hung to her tiny waist. Now barely twenty-five years old, she had worry lines around her eyes and a rapidly expanding waist line. Her hair was piled on top of her head in a messy bun, its once rich blackness now showing a splattering of premature gray.

A tentative knock at the front door interrupted Isabella's attention to the noise coming from Carlos's room. It was Maria with a sleeping twin in each arm, bundled in blankets even though it was an unseasonably warm October morning in Texas.

"Hola," Maria said with false cheer, peering into the apartment. She handed Isabella the babies.

"How is Carlos feeling today?" Maria whispered with a strained smile, her eyes nervously perusing the apartment for any evidence of his tirades.

31

"He is fine, Maria, just resting in his room," Isabella said quickly, wishing Maria would leave before another crashing sound came from Carlos's room, before he screamed as if he was being tortured, before he ran from his room and lunged at them in anger, his little arms flailing in the air.

Maria seemed satisfied with that answer.

"I will be back at five to pick up the little ones," she said as she bent over and gave each sleeping baby a kiss on the cheek before she left.

Isabella closed the door behind Maria and then jumped at the sound of Carlos's sudden scream.

Holy Mary, give me strength, she silently prayed. She headed towards Carlos's room with the sleeping twins in her arms and then thought better of that. She quickly placed each twin in the two white cribs she kept in the front room before she walked towards Carlos's room again. The door was closed.

"Carlos my baby, what is the matter?" Isabella whispered as she gingerly opened his door. Carlos stood naked in the middle of his bedroom, his pull-up diaper discarded and tossed in a corner. He screamed again and then stared at Isabella with brown eyes that were wide yet empty, devoid of any emotional connection to her. Fecal matter was smeared on his face, in his hair, and trailed down his legs. Isabella felt like screaming herself as she covered her face with her hands. Carlos wasn't potty trained yet. She had tried in vain to teach him to use the toilet, but she couldn't get him to understand that he needed to sit on the toilet as soon as he felt the urge to use the bathroom. She stared wordlessly at her son for a few moments and then as the stench of his feces permeated the air, she snapped into action.

"Carlos, go to the bathroom. I will give you a shower," she said quickly, hoping the twins wouldn't wake up before she was finished cleaning him.

Carlos obeyed and as he walked across his carpeted bedroom floor to the bathroom, she noticed the feces on his feet as he left small brown footprints on the light tan carpet. Isabella wondered if she had any carpet cleaner left in the house. It was so expensive, about four or five dollars a bottle. Isabella carefully walked to the small window in his room and opened it, grateful for the smell of the fresh Texas October air. She leaned out the window and breathed in the fresh air again, the warm breeze gently caressing her face. She closed her eyes. Next year, Carlos would be five. The large public school down the street had a kindergarten class for children like him. He would spend the morning in school and would only be home in the afternoon. Isabella guiltily admitted to herself that she could not wait for this day to come. A scream from the bathroom jolted her back into reality.

"I am coming, Carlos," Isabella called and as she rushed across the room to the bathroom, she stepped in a pile of feces. She grimaced as she glanced at the bottom of her shoes before she walked into bathroom. Carlos was violently rocking back and forth as he stood in the middle of the bathtub, repetitively rubbing his feces covered hands on the shower curtain.

Isabella reached around him and turned on the shower. Carlos clapped his hands excitedly, his eyelids fluttering as the warm water cascaded through his hair and down his back. Isabella smiled for the first time today. Carlos loved taking showers. It vaguely occurred to Isabella that his toileting accidents might not be so accidental after all, that the accidents might be Carlos's way of taking as many showers as he wanted.

"I am glad you like your shower, Carlos," she said as she picked up a bar of soap and began to wash the feces from his hair and body. Just then she heard the sound of the babies crying in the front room. Isabella sighed as she used a wet hand to push back a trickle of sweat.

"Carlos, please enjoy your shower while I check on Maria's babies. I will be back soon, okay?" Isabella looked at her son. His eyes were closed and his once violent rocking had changed to gently rocking on his heels, his head leaned back as the water hit his face. Sometimes Isabella wished she could leave Carlos in the shower all day, the only place he truly seemed at peace. However, the water bill would be too high and Manuel would rant and rave like a crazy man.

Isabella left Carlos in the shower as she sat in the front room and rocked the babies until their cries turned to soft cooing. She looked at the clock on the wall. It was almost 7:30 am, time to feed the babies. Isabella gently laid the twins back into their cribs and walked into the kitchen, where she retrieved two bottles of formula from the refrigerator and heated them in the bottle warmer. Just as she was walked into the front room with the heated bottles, Isabella heard a blood curdling scream coming from the bathroom. The babies were frightened by the sound and started to cry. Isabella dropped the bottles on the floor and ran to the bathroom.

Steam was coming from the shower. Carlos was flailing at the water as he backed into a corner of the tub, his terrified screams filling the small bathroom. His brown skin was red and blistery from hot water.

"My God!" Isabella shrieked as she turned the water off. She wasn't sure if Carlos had turned the water to hot or if something had malfunctioned.

Isabella lifted Carlos from the shower and wrapped him in a towel. He screamed at the touch of her hands against his tender sore skin. His screams blended with the cries of the hungry babies coming from the front room.

Isabella tried to carry Carlos into the front room as he struggled in her arms and clawed at her face with his tiny hands.

"Carlos, stop," she pleaded. He escaped from her grasp and ran to a corner of the room, where he huddled naked, rubbing his reddened skin. He rocked back and forth, his eyes staring at nothing.

The babies were lying on their backs and staring up at her from their cribs, still crying for their bottles.

"Okay Jose and Cristina, I will feed you now or maybe you are wet and need your diapers changed," Isabella rambled as she blindly searched for the bottles she had dropped. Her temples were pulsating from tension and fatigue, her cheeks stinging from Carlos's hands.

Her own hands were shaking. She barely heard the urgent knocking on her front door.

"Isabella, are you there? Open the door. It is me, Lena."

Isabella recognized her older sister's voice and quickly opened the door. She was so relieved to see Lena she gave her a tight hug.

"Lena, what are you doing here? Why are you not at work?"

Lena sighed as she stepped inside the apartment.

"The restaurant has let me go," she said, shaking her head. "Times are very bad, Isabella. The restaurant cannot even afford to keep me on to clean their bathrooms."

Lena stopped talking as she took in the chaos around her, Carlos red and crouching in a corner screaming, the twins crying as they lay in their cribs, the stench of Carlos's feces lingering in the air.

Lena spoke briskly as she immediately took over.

"Isabella, you take care of the babies. I will take care of Carlos."

As Isabella sat on the couch and fed the babies, she watched as Lena gently swaddled Carlos in his towel and applied cocoa butter to his skin. Carlos lay quietly in Lena's arms, his eyes closed, his breathing even. Isabella marveled at how calm Carlos became in Lena's presence. She had initially felt a little resentment when she first noticed the calming effect Lena had on Carlos, something she began to notice last year. Today, she felt nothing but relief that Lena was helping her.

The two sisters sat in silence taking care of the children. Finally, Isabella spoke.

"What will you do for work, Lena?"

Lena shrugged as she stroked Carlos's soft black hair, still wet from the shower.

"I will find a job at another restaurant or maybe I will clean houses like Maria," Lena said, glancing at the twins.

Isabella sighed. "Do you ever think about going home? Going home to Mexico?"

Lena gave a contemptuous snort. Lena didn't care for Manuel, didn't like the way he treated Carlos, but the one thing they had in common was a shared pride of living in America.

"Never," she spat. "I miss our family but I want to stay in America. Here I will find another job tomorrow. In Mexico, there is no hope for a better life."

"I miss home," Isabella said softly. Lena was right. It was harder to survive economically in Mexico, but Isabella didn't care about that. She missed her mama's soothing voice and comforting hugs and her papa's hearty jokes. She longed for her grandmama's cooking and her grandpapa's colorful stories of growing up in Mexico as a little boy.

The phone in Isabella's apartment rang. Isabella glanced at the caller ID, a luxury Manuel insisted on having as protection against answering the phone for any unwanted callers. It was Manuel calling from his cell phone. He was working a landscaping job only three blocks away from their apartment today and had forgotten his thermos filled with cold papaya juice.

Isabella sighed. "That is no problem. Lena is with me. We will pack up the children and be there soon."

Manuel grunted his disapproval. "Lena is with you? Why is she there? Why is she not working?"

"I will tell you later, Manuel," Isabella said before she hung up. "Manuel needs his thermos," she called over her shoulder to Lena as she walked to the kitchen and retrieved the thermos from the refrigerator.

Lena rolled her eyes as she carried Carlos into his room to dress him.

"That man of yours. He will forget his own name if you do not tell him. He is no smarter than Carlos."

Isabella was silent as she placed the twins in an old double stroller that Maria had bought at a yard sale for two dollars. There was no love loss between her sister and her husband, no need for Isabella to respond.

Lena returned a short time later with Carlos in her arms. Carlos was dressed in blue jeans and a sweatshirt. He was sucking his thumb and making quiet, contented noises as he gazed lovingly at his aunt.

Isabella shook her head in disbelief. "How do you do it, Lena?" she asked. "How do you make him so calm?"

Lena smiled as she looked down at her nephew. They smiled at each other and then Lena kissed the top of his head.

"I do not have an answer for you, Isabella," she said. "Maybe he can feel my love. I am so crazy about him, you know. Maybe he knows I have no little babies of my own to love and feels sorry for me."

Lena was unmarried and had no children. She was waiting for the right man, she told everyone who was curious as to why she was still single. Isabella admired her sister. Lena didn't care what anyone thought and refused to let anyone's inquiries pressure her into making a hasty decision about marriage and children. Manuel liked to laugh at Lena behind her back and frequently called her *Lena lesbiana*.

"No man will put up with your sister," he enjoyed saying to Isabella. "She is too headstrong, too macho."

Isabella and Lena left the apartment with the children in tow. Isabella pushed the double stroller while Carlos walked alongside Lena, holding her hand. It was a warm and sunny day in Texas, even in October. Several of the yards they passed had flowers of many colors still in full bloom. Isabella glanced at the flowers as she enjoyed the soothing warm breeze caress her face. Her thoughts drifted to Mexico once again. There were so many colorful flowers in Mexico and some even grew very tall.

"What do you think mama and papa are doing right now?" she asked softly.

Lena shrugged. "They are wasting their time sitting on their old porch, laughing at something that is not even funny."

Lena peered at her sister through narrowed eyes. She spoke harshly. "You must stop thinking about Mexico. You are in America now. You must make a good life for yourself here."

Isabella and Lena arrived at Manuel's work site. When Manuel saw Isabella, he grinned broadly and walked over, sweat pouring down his face from working in the sun. He ignored Lena and Carlos as he took the thermos from Isabella. He opened it and gulped his papaya juice and then wiped his mouth with the back of his hand.

"Thank you, Isabella," he said. "That was so good. Like the Americans say, that hit the spot." He chuckled at his own comment before he walked away and resumed working. As Isabella and Lena turned to leave with the children, the noise of a leaf blower from the work site filled the air. Carlos covered his ears with hands and emitted ear deafening screams. Some of the other laborers abruptly stopped working and looked questioningly at Manuel as a terrified Carlos began to punch Isabella with his fists while he continued to scream.

"Stop it, Carlos," Isabella pleaded, trying to block his blows. She looked desperately at Lena. "Help me get him out of here before Manuel gets angry," she said breathlessly but it was too late. Manuel was taking off his belt as he charged towards his son, his face swollen with rage. Lena faced Manuel bravely as Isabella tried to drag Carlos away.

"No!" Lena shouted, her arms outstretched towards Manuel in protest. "We are leaving now. Go back to work, Manuel!"

Manuel drew back his fist and punched Lena in the face so hard she fell to the ground. "I am so sick of you and that boy, Lena!" he raged, standing over her with clenched fists. "I will teach you both some manners!" Manuel then stormed towards Carlos and grabbed him by the arm, whipping him savagely with his belt. Lena staggered to her feet but was too dazed from Manuel's punch to remain standing and crumpled to the ground again. Isabella tried to grab the belt from Manuel.

"Stop beating my son!" she screamed at the top of her lungs. She looked desperately at the other workers. "Help my son," she begged but no one moved as all fearful eyes were fixed on Manuel. The workers were all illegals and afraid to intervene should the cops arrive, terrified at the prospect of deportation.

Manuel pushed Isabella away and kept whipping Carlos, who by now was lying on the ground next to his aunt curled in the fetal position, barely able to emit even a whimper as his small body was repeatedly lashed with the belt. Isabella saw the blank mask of rage on her husband's sweaty face as he stood over his son, administering a seemingly endless beating. He had whipped Carlos many times before in their apartment but had never before attacked him with such unrelenting brutality. It suddenly occurred to Isabella that Manuel was angrier this time because he felt publicly humiliated, because his own son had dared to lay a finger on *his* wife in front of the men with whom he worked. *Machismo*, Lena had often said slyly in reference to Manuel. Suddenly, Isabella's mind was very clear as she knew with a sobering finality what she had to do. She felt calm, almost in a trancelike state as she walked over to the worker holding the leaf blower that had started this whole catastrophe, the sound of the belt striking flesh ringing louder and louder in her ears until her mind was numb with resolve.

"Give me this, please," she said, taking the leaf blower from the worker who was too startled to protest. She held the leaf blower over her head as she calmly walked back over to Manuel, who in his rage never saw her coming.

"I told you to stop beating my son," she said quietly before she brought the leaf blower down onto Manuel's head with all the strength she could muster over and over again. Somewhere in the distance she heard voices shouting at her to stop. Manuel stared at her wordlessly, his eyes blank and cloudy. He clutched the hem of her dress as he dropped heavily to his knees. Finally his eyes closed as he toppled over on one side and lay still.

***

Isabella received four visitors in one day. Her papa and grandpapa greeted her with effusive hugs while her mama and grandmama wiped away tears.

"One year in this place will go by very fast, you shall see," her papa said bravely. Her mama nodded as she dabbed her eyes with a worn tissue.

"Carlos is fine, Isabella. Lena is taking very good care of him. She tells him every day how brave you are and how much you love him. She is raising him as if he were her own son."

Isabella smiled. "I am so happy to hear that. I know Carlos will be fine. Lena loves him so very much."

Isabella's grandmama spoke timidly. "Isabella, after you are released from jail, you will never be able to return to America because of the deportation. You must stay here in Mexico. Carlos will live with Lena. She will raise Carlos in America."

The four looked at Isabella tentatively, not sure how she would respond to the news.

Isabella smiled peacefully. "I am so happy to be back in Mexico, even if I must serve one year in jail. Carlos is better off with Lena. He loves her more than anyone. I have always known that."

Isabella's grandpapa spoke. "Lena tells us that Manuel is getting better. He doesn't talk so good and his words do not always make sense, but he has moved on. He has an American woman now. He has moved in with her and she is taking good care of him. He cannot work too much because of the headaches, but his woman is taking care of him. Lena says Manuel does not know who Carlos is. He does not remember he has a son."

Isabella nodded slowly with relief before she spoke softly. "Manuel is just like Carlos now."

Everyone was quiet and then Isabella's mama gave her a hug. "I am very sorry for what has become of Manuel but I am so very proud of you, Isabella. You protected your son."

Isabella's grandpapa suddenly clapped his hands as a jovial smile spread across his face. "We are all too serious today. Our Isabella is home! Isabella, have you heard the joke about the rooster from Mexico?"

After he told the joke, the five of them sat in the visitor's room of the jail and laughed and laughed despite the fact that the joke was not even funny.

# Holiday Girl

Flight 316 glided smoothly through the air, its final destination sunny Los Angeles. Janie Holliday sat back in her comfortable first class seat with her IPod and smiled expectantly at the blonde flight attendant who was sauntering down the aisle offering complimentary drinks. The flight attendant's lips moved and then her mouth spread into a smile revealing perfectly straight white teeth that contrasted sharply with the bronze color of her skin, probably the result of many visits to a tanning salon.

"Scotch, please," Janie requested automatically even though she couldn't hear what the flight attendant was saying above the jazz music drifting from her IPod. When the scotch was handed to her, Janie took a sip and leaned back in her chair, closing her eyes as each movement of the plane brought her closer to what had become her favorite city, her personal "sin" city. Her reasons for flying to Los Angeles once a month were less than honorable but she felt no shame. Shame had disappeared long ago, replaced with an intense need to enjoy life in the moment, to experience the pleasures that awaited her, to leave no stone unturned in her quest for personal fulfillment. It would have been convenient for her to use her lousy husband and troubled teenage sons as an excuse for the extramarital affair that she was having, but no such excuse existed. Her husband Peter was quiet, gainfully employed, and tried his best to be emotionally available at least some of the time. Her sons were straight A students with impeccable manners. The urge for unbridled passion and excitement had begun in her early forties and at age forty-nine, it showed no sign of stopping.

Janie's friends didn't appear to be experiencing this kind of mid-life crisis. They were either contentedly settled in the routine of humdrum marital life or were peaceful divorcees, fully recovered from the wounds of former marriages gone wrong. Janie thought that her youthful appearance, which she thought belied her chronological age by at least ten years was the culprit, the reason for her restless spirit. Janie was slender and very petite, not an inch over five feet tall with flawless cocoa brown skin and long black hair that was bone straight due to regular Dominican blow-outs. Any gray hair she had was carefully concealed by professionally applied hair color. Her eyes were big and brown, luminous like a sex goddess yet innocent like the eyes of a little girl. Janie's ageless beauty attracted men of all ages, of all races, from all walks of life. This had once been a source of pride for her husband of almost nineteen years but over the years Peter had eventually grown to find the never ending attention Janie received annoying to no end. Janie thought that perhaps Peter's annoyance sprang from a little bit of envy in that he looked every bit of his forty-nine years.

"Wish we could just go somewhere once in a while without every Tom, Dick, and Harry looking at you," he would remark, trying to sound casual. "Don't know, makes me feel like I should be defending your honor or something."

Janie would smile and tell him she only had eyes for him while wondering if Peter knew that wasn't even remotely true. It was true that while she could care less about all the nameless men who stared at her the minute she walked into a room there was one man she cared very much about, one young man who had captured her heart and refused to let it go.

***

Samuel Somerville thought his name made him sound old and preferred to be called by the more affable sounding Sam. He was born and raised in Los Angeles and had never wanted to live anywhere else. He didn't mind no-frills living which was strange considering the fact that he lived in one of the most expensive cities in the country, but somehow he managed to survive. Sam's efficiency apartment was rent-controlled and he drove a Ford Fiesta with more than a few miles on it. Sam's apartment was also home to his dog Grover and his cat that he had named Kit Kat in honor of his favorite candy. His Brazilian twenty-four year old girlfriend Carla was a part-time model and harpist who crashed at his apartment a few days a week between modeling assignments and paying musical venues. Sam was also a part-time model and part-time server in an upscale restaurant in Beverly Hills. He was twenty-eight years old and just as gorgeous, if not more so, than both Carla and his married lover Janie who lived in Arizona but flew into Los Angeles about once a month to see him. Sam was the product of a half-white, half-Peruvian mother and an African American father. He stood six feet four inches tall, his height inherited from his former pro-basketball player father. He had caramel colored skin and curly brown hair, and his grey eyes were inquisitive yet alluring. Because of his lean muscular physique, most of the calls his agent received on his behalf were offers to model men's underwear. Sam didn't mind at all. Modeling men's underwear paid the bills while giving him a chance to show off his perfect body to the world, something he never tired of doing.

It was a clear and sunny June morning in Los Angeles. As Sam lounged in bed with Grover and Kit Kat sleeping nearby, he vaguely remembered that Janie Holliday was coming to town today. He started calling her 'Holiday Girl' after meeting her at a Christmas party in Phoenix last year where he had been booked for a photo shoot. As easygoing and fun-loving as he was, Sam hated the holidays, Christmas in particular. It seemed too commercial, too concentrated on buying expensive gifts and trying to make people happy by spending exorbitant amounts of money. Sam could barely afford to buy anything for anyone and hated to admit that while his simple lifestyle caused him less stress, it left no room for excess spending either. Holiday Girl had brightened his impoverished Christmas by getting great sex from a beautiful older woman whose sex drive was unmatched by any woman his age that he had ever slept with. Married women were especially passionate between the sheets, usually desperate to be touched by someone new, starving to make love to a man with whom they didn't have to share the drudgeries of everyday life. After the holidays ended and the New Year began his mood lifted so it wouldn't have fazed him at all if Holiday Girl had decided to stop seeing him but she kept flying into Los Angeles every month. Who was he to complain about the best sex of his life flying into town, no expense incurred by him? He was always careful and made sure her visits occurred when Carla was safely out of town on a photo shoot. He loved Carla and knew that once he was ready to make a commitment to settle down and forsake all others, she would be his wife.

***

Janie's flight from Phoenix to Los Angeles was about an hour. Her usual routine was to fly to Sam's place once a month on a Friday evening immediately after work and return home on Sunday afternoon, wearing her invisible cloak of shame that she was convinced Peter and her teenage sons could see. Spending a weekend of shopping with her college gal pals was the excuse that she had been using for the past six months, ever since she had met Sam Somerville at a Christmas party hosted by an acquaintance of a colleague who was famous for bringing together eclectic groups of people ranging from conservative CEOs to flamboyant models and quirky artists, B-list actors, and cut-throat Hollywood type executives. Janie was a gallery director for a famous art museum and was regularly invited to parties and social events. Meeting new people was a customary part of her life but meeting Sam was special from the start. He was sexy as hell, laid back to a fault, yet grimly fatalistic like most twenty-somethings. The combination of these personality traits drove her wild both in and out of bed. Janie was more than willing to fly out to see him more than once a month but he wouldn't let her. My work schedule is so chaotic, he kept saying as he promised to let her know when things slowed down a bit. Janie never pressed the issue because she didn't want to anger him into cutting her out of his life. She could tell by Sam's sparse apartment and the hoopty he drove that money was tight for him, modeling assignments had to be taken immediately when offered, and they almost always involved travel. Thus far Janie had visited Sam a total of five times and during each visit she would give him several hundred dollars to help him get by even though he never asked her for the money but always accepted it without hesitation. He promised to pay her back but she knew he never would and truth be told, she didn't want him to. Janie wanted Sam to need her for something because she simply had to be needed by him. She could tell by his guttural moans and the almost violent way that his body trembled as he exploded inside of her that he loved sleeping with her but Janie was no fool. This was not Phoenix where women with her looks were less common. In Los Angeles she was one pretty face in a sea of many beautiful women who were happy to sleep with a man as gorgeous as Sam, most of them decades younger than she. Janie's infatuation for Sam went well beyond the mere physical. The first time she saw him she knew she had to have him in her life no matter what the price.

***

Sam met Holiday Girl at a Christmas party in Phoenix that he almost didn't attend because after a day of working under hot lights and flashing cameras in his eyes, all he wanted to do was go back to his hotel, text Carla, and get some sleep. At the last minute his booking agent insisted that he go to the party.

"You must be seen everywhere, you're fabulous," crooned his agent, a white woman in her mid-fifties with spiky orange hair and big black glasses that virtually covered her entire wrinkled face. True to form, in the next breath she managed to insult him. "My dear, time is of the essence. You're twenty-eight years old and growing a tad long in the tooth for this industry, my darling."

Sam was used to his agent and how quickly she changed from complimentary to insulting. She was his old mean girl, he often said jokingly to himself. While it was true that he was approaching thirty, Sam knew he could easily pass for a man in his early twenties and often did when he was booked for jobs. Sam wasn't short on self-confidence and was comfortable in his own skin. When he saw Holiday Girl at the party he could tell right away that while she was beautifully well-preserved she was probably about fifty but that wasn't going to stop him from putting on the moves. An attractive cougar alone at a party filled with young people was there for one reason only.  She was looking to get laid and Sam knew he was the man for the job.  When their eyes met across the room, the come hither look in her eyes clinched the deal before one word was ever spoken.

***

Janie glanced at her small diamond Rolex watch and wondered if she should buy Sam a matching Rolex.  She was due to arrive at Los Angeles International Airport in less than thirty minutes.  She sipped her scotch.  Sam had a lot of pride so he probably would never accept a lavish gift from her.  She stared out the window.  In her peripheral vision she could see a tan-skinned man in the row adjacent to hers who appeared to be in his sixties with sleek silver hair.  His tailored business suit was the same color as his hair.  Like most men who saw her, his gaze was admiring and filled with hope that she would offer him at least a glance.  Janie pretended not to notice him as she wondered if Sam missed her as much as she missed him when they weren't together.  It was becoming increasingly hard to remain married to Peter when she was in love with another man.  Her sons no longer occupied her time to the extent that she was able to ignore the sad fact that her marriage was a farce. Her sons were teenagers and concerned only with school, sports, and their friends. When the boys weren't home which was often these days, Janie and Peter barely spoke and were rarely ever in the same room.  Janie squared her shoulders with resolve as she drained her glass of scotch. She couldn't take it anymore, this half-life she was living, the lie that her life had become to maintain the appearances of a union that should have ended years ago.  When she returned home this time, she was going to tell Peter she wanted a divorce.  He could have the house and joint custody of the boys. Janie knew Sam wasn't ready to get married just yet.  He was vested almost solely in his career but she would wait for him and would even support him financially if she had to. Even if he never married her, Janie didn't care.  She would take him any way she could get him, even if it meant being a mere live-in girlfriend.  In all the nineteen years she had been married to Peter, she had never felt an ounce of the unbridled passion and devotion she felt for Sam.

"Would you like another?"

Janie ignored the voice for a moment then glanced at the silver haired man who was smiling and gesturing towards her empty glass.

"No, thank you," she answered politely. She looked out the window again, hoping the move would signal the end of any conversation before it began.

"You look like a lady with a plan," the man said, his voice baritone and heavy. Janie glanced at his hands. His large hands belied the pampered life his expensive clothes implied. His hands were calloused and scarred, his knuckles bruised. The man noticed Janie's glance and laughed.

"Former boxer," he explained as he looked at his hands admiringly, spreading his thick massive fingers. "Won a lot of fights with these hands but that was a long time ago."

Janie nodded politely and leaned back in her seat. She closed her eyes, hoping the man would stop talking.

"Travel to LA often?" he asked after a brief silence. Janie sighed as she opened her eyes again.

"Not really," she said abruptly, missing Sam even more. Sam was so different from other men in that he was never slow to take a hint. In her eyes, Sam was perfection. He was her *everything*.

"Aha," the man said. "Where are you from?"

Janie gave him an incredulous stare. "Excuse me?" she asked sharply.

The man laughed self-consciously. "Sorry," he apologized. "It's just that when I see a pretty lady I want to get to know her."

Janie relaxed, feeling bad for snapping at the man. "It's okay," she relented. "I'm from Arizona."

The man nodded. "You're lucky. It's a short flight for you. Surprised your husband doesn't mind you traveling alone, beautiful as you are. Your husband is one lucky fellow to have a woman like you."

Janie glanced at the wedding band on her finger that would soon be tucked away in her purse. She felt a sudden pang of guilt and wondered if she was feeling that way because the man said that Peter was lucky to have her or because the wedding band would soon disappear from her finger for the next two days. Janie never wore her wedding ring when she was with Sam. She liked to pretend she was free to love him and the ring was a painful reminder that she wasn't. Janie allowed herself a little smile. She would be free after she told Peter she wanted a divorce. The wedding band would never grip her finger like a cruel albatross ever again.

"So how old are you?" the man was asking. "Mid-forties?"

Janie bristled at the insinuation that she looked a day over thirty-nine. "Why?" she asked tersely. "Do I look that old?"

The man realized his gaffe and laughed self-consciously for the second time since the dialogue began. "Hey, mid-forties seems young to an old geezer like me," he explained. "I'm sixty-two. Migrated from Spain many years ago with my parents when I was only three. Don't speak a lick of Spanish, sad to say."

The man beckoned to the flight attendant. "Another drink for the beautiful *young* lady," he said. "So," he smiled, turning back to Janie. "Let's start over again. My name is Santiago." He proffered a scarred hand that when Janie extended hers, enveloped her small hand completely. She felt his callouses against her skin.

"Janie," she said. Santiago was about to say something else when the plane suddenly jolted. Janie looked startled as Santiago laughed.

"You really need that drink," he joked. "It's just a little turbulence. We should be landing in about fifteen minutes."

After the flight attendant brought Janie her second glass of scotch, the perfunctory announcement was made about seat backs and placing folding trays in their full upright position. Janie felt her excitement growing as she did each time she was about to arrive in Los Angeles. She couldn't wait to grab her carry on luggage which consisted of two bags and hurry through the airport to pick up the rental car that she had reserved. The nagging thought that Sam had never once offered to pick her up from the airport any time she came to visit him was shoved in the part of her brain that denied every less than honorable aspect of him and recognized only the good.

"Better finish that drink," Santiago was saying. "We're about to land."

Janie gulped her scotch and instantly felt light-headed. "Whew," she exclaimed softly and closed her eyes, letting the liquor flow through her brain, through her body, encasing her loins. She suddenly felt aroused. Sam was going to get it good tonight, she thought with a grin. She couldn't wait to feel his lean young body beside hers, on top of hers. His smell, his touch, his guttural moans were worth the trips to Los Angeles. Janie suddenly realized with finality that while she wanted Peter to have the very best that life had to offer and certainly wished him no harm, she no longer cared about him the way a wife should care about her husband. She hoped her boys would understand that their mom needed to be happy and would respect her decision to share the second half of her life with her one and only true love. She felt the wheels touch down on the runway but the scotch was dulling her senses, her perception of what was going on around her. Janie wondered why the flight attendants were suddenly racing through the aisles, their once serene faces tense and frightened. Santiago's tan face was suddenly red, his strong hands gripping the armrests until blue veins were straining against his skin. Passengers were screaming, crying, cursing, praying as the plane suddenly jolted violently from side to side and increased in speed. The plane is on the runway so it should be slowing down, Janie thought slowly. The empty glass she held in her hand crashed to the floor.

"Oh sweet Jesus," Santiago moaned as he stared at her, the terror in his eyes coupled with the chaos on the plane thrusting her out of her scotch induced haze. He clutched his heart as his chest and legs began to convulse, his reddened face sweaty, his eyes wide from terror and pain. He gasped for air as his eyes blinked repeatedly then fixed on nothing. Santiago's mouth was agape, his body still.

"Santiago!" Janie screamed but her voice was drowned out by the terrified sounds of everyone around her as passengers were thrown into the aisle and into windows, slammed into the hard seats. Screams of horror turned into moans of despair. Thoughts of Sam were forgotten as the tail section of the plane and the first class detached from the middle of the plane amidst the sounds of screeching metal. As the fragmented parts of the plane continued to slide out of control at an alarming speed down the runway, the film of her life played clearly through her mind. Janie could see her first date with Peter, their wedding, the lavish honeymoon in Barbados, herself as an expectant mom. In her mind's eye, she saw her boys as toddlers taking their first steps, their baby teeth as white as pearls, clapping their hands as they sang nursery rhymes, playing in the front yard, going to school for the very first time. She sobbed as she prayed for her life to be spared, to return to the sanctity of her home, to see her boys again.

***

One year after the plane crash, Sam and his pregnant fiancée exchanged wedding vows on the beach one quiet June evening, their wedding attended by a justice of the peace, Sam's cranky booking agent, his pets Grover and Kit Kat, and the beautiful sunset overlooking the still blue water. Had Holiday Girl not named him sole beneficiary of her quarter million dollar travel life insurance policy, he would still be driving a hoopty, living in an efficiency apartment, and waiting for the day he could afford to marry Carla, his one and only true love.

# Margaret "Amber" Owens

**O**ne rainy Sunday morning in May, residents of the tiny town of Brookville, Wyoming listened to Reverend John T. Owens as he stood before his congregation and preached a sermon about what he considered to be the greatest two sins of the world. Fornication and homosexuality; those were always the subject of his sermons when the good reverend preached, his booming voice filling the tiny Fundamentalist church attended by most of the people who lived in Brookville, population two hundred. Margaret Owens sat in the pews as she listened to her father preach. She looked at her father through narrowed eyes, wondering why his sermons were always based on what he called sexual deviancy. Why not preach about the substance abuse which plagued so many of her high school peers? What about teen depression and suicide, uncertainty about the future, rising unemployment rates? As far as she was concerned, those were real problems that needed to be discussed. Margaret knew that the so-called sins her father preached about could never be controlled. As long as people had hormones and sexual urges they would continue to have sex and no one could stop them, not even her father, no matter how powerful he considered himself to be. Reverend Owens ruled both his church and his household with an iron fist, leaving virtually nothing open for debate. Her mother Winifred and fifteen year old brother Joshua had lived under his tyrannical thumb for so long their minds were like mush, their heads moving like Bobblehead dolls with their incessant nods of agreement with every ridiculous notion that came into her father's head.

Margaret was very different from both her mother and brother, which was always a point of contention in the Owens' household. She hated her father but had learned to feign passivity to some extent, her pretense borne from a sense of survival. Margaret had grown weary of the many painful and degrading trips to the woodshed in their backyard where after her father had ordered her to lift her dress and pull down her underwear, she would receive ten unbearable whacks on her backside with a wooden paddle while he read an assortment of scriptures from the Bible. While Margaret and her father shared no common beliefs, they looked amazingly alike with the same red hair, ice blue eyes, and pale freckled skin. Margaret's hair was long and wiry, streaming down her back like a fiery mane. She hated her hair and longed to have it cut and styled at the local beauty parlor but her father wouldn't hear of it. "A woman's hair is her crowning glory," he chanted like a drone. When she was twelve years old, she had experienced an especially painful trip to the woodshed after stealing her mother's sewing scissors and chopping her hair to her shoulders. "Never cut your hair again," her father had panted after he finished administering the punishment, dropping the paddle in exhaustion.

Over the course of time, her mother and brother had come to share his same strict beliefs and barely even spoke to her anymore. Margaret could care less. She had no respect for those two creatures; they were like aliens to her. She thanked God that this was her last month of high school and she would turn eighteen the following month. Unbeknownst to her family, she was applying for admission to dozens of universities as far away from Wyoming as she could get, the money for application fees derived from what she had earned and saved by working after school jobs in Brookville since she was thirteen. She knew her father would never agree to pay for an out-of-state college which to him would mean losing control over her but she didn't care. Her grades were good and she was a solid test taker, which meant that she would probably ace the SAT and be a strong candidate for a full academic scholarship. After she was accepted to a university, Margaret knew she would never return to Wyoming or see her family ever again. Once she left Wyoming, Margaret also planned to legally change her first name to Amber. The name appealed to her because it meant both perfect jewel and a reddish-orange color, just like her hair. Her father had named her Margaret in honor of her paternal grandmother, a large woman of few words and a permanent frown etched on her face who died when Margaret was seven.

She was especially interested in applying to universities in New York, a place that brought to mind bright lights, artistic people, independent thinkers, and fashion galore. After she arrived in New York, one of the first things she planned to do was throw away the plain below the knee length gingham dresses that her mother made on her old rickety sewing machine and that her father insisted she wear. She would buy as many pairs of slacks as she could afford, cut her hair in a short sassy bob and become Amber Owens of New York.

***

Nineteen-year old Linh Tran was an only child, not because her parents hadn't tried to have more children, but because her mother was suddenly rendered infertile for reasons unknown and was never able to conceive again. Linh migrated with her parents from Vietnam to New York City when she was three years old and sixteen years later considered herself to be a seasoned New York girl, a fashionista, pouring through every fashion magazine she could get her hands on. She was petite and very chic with jet black hair cut in a short spiky style and dark almond shaped eyes. After graduating from high school, Linh started taking classes part-time in fashion design and business administration at the City College of New York. She also worked part-time at a chic little boutique in the Manhattan borough of New York City known as the garment district. Her parents were bitterly disappointed in her career choice and expected her to get married, have children, and work at the tiny nail salon her family owned and staffed with Vietnamese immigrants, many of them her equally judgmental and miserable cousins. Linh didn't care what her parents or her jealous cousins thought. She worked at the salon for exactly one week until she decided she loathed the smell of the chemicals used in the salon to create acrylic fingernails. The mindless routine of the job was unbearable to her which consisted of painting nails and scrubbing feet, too many of the feet bloated and grotesque in her opinion. Linh had a dream for herself that absolutely did not include working at or even one day owning the family nail salon. It wasn't enough for Linh to merely work in a boutique, either. Her ultimate dream was to own a clothing boutique in the garment district. She would Americanize her first name and call her boutique *Lynn Tran Clothing*. She was determined to make her dream happen and refused to let her family or anyone else stop her.

***

Margaret turned eighteen and graduated from high school on a hot day in June. As usual her family was stoic at the graduation, barely even uttering congratulations. She received no gifts from her family, no celebratory dinner, and when the good reverend, her mother and brother fell asleep that night, Margaret crept into her parents' room. As she stood over their bed looking down at her mother and father, she felt empty, felt nothing at all. Her mother was curled on her side in the fetal position while her father lay on his back emitting loud snores, his reading glasses and bible resting on his chest that rose and fell with each thunderous breath he took. She crept from her parents' bedroom and went into her brother's room. Joshua was in his bed curled up in the fetal position just like her mother, barely making a sound as he slept. She left his room and went back to her own bedroom where she packed one bag, its contents including her acceptance letter to the City College of New York. Margaret Owens never looked back as she climbed out of her bedroom window, walked to the bus station and boarded a greyhound bus, destination Manhattan.

***

It was the end of September on the campus of the City College of New York and Linh sat in her Business 101 class. When she spotted the girl who by sheer luck was seated in front of her, Linh realized the girl had the reddest hair she had ever seen and her short bobbed cut was fierce. Linh quickly perused the girl from head to toe as well as she could from where she was seated and felt a familiar pang that she had long ago gave up pushing down, suppressing, ignoring. Linh had first acted on the feeling at age fifteen and imagined that her ultra conservative Vietnamese family would keel over from utter shock if they knew the truth. The thought made her smile broadly.

Amber Owens sat in her Business 101 class, completely unaware that she was being watched. Even though she was deeply engrossed in the lecture and deliriously happy just to be sitting in a class at City College, she couldn't help but let her thoughts shift for a moment as she touched her short hair. It felt so good to be forever relieved of the long hair that used to hang like burdensome heavy curtains around her face, her so-called crowning glory. She glanced down at her pants, her white shirt, and stylish loafers. Amber smiled. Never again would she ever be caught dead in a dress or a skirt. She felt so 'right', as if her life had just begun. Her full scholarship to City College covered all school related expenses, so Amber was able to use the money she had saved from her after-school jobs to have her hair cut the second she arrived in New York. She also purchased an assortment of reasonably priced slacks, white shirts, and loafer shoes. She hadn't legally changed her first name yet but she knew in her heart and soul who she was every time she painstakingly wrote the name Margaret or whenever a professor called her by that ghastly name. She was Amber.

***

Linh still lived at home not because she wanted to but out of sheer financial necessity. Linh was desperate for money and at this point in her life, there was little she wouldn't do to make a quick buck, even agreeing to do a little snooping around for some old guy she met online in a religious chat room. She loved to hang out in the religious chat rooms because she had met some of her best lovers there, confused people looking for a wild girl like her to free them from their sexual inhibitions. She couldn't afford to live on campus and certainly didn't have enough money to rent a decent place off-campus. Her mother and father refused to help her pay rent, instead preferring that she live at home so they could keep an eye on her.

Linh was so desperate to move out of her parents' home that she was seriously considering moving into one of the many homeless shelters in New York to get away from their stifling morality and their rigid traditional Vietnamese beliefs. Linh's thoughts were interrupted when the professor dismissed class. The girl with the red hair gathered her books and stood up and for a moment her ice blue eyes met Linh's jet black eyes. Linh offered a tentative smile. The girl looked at her for a moment before her thin lips slowly spread into a small rigid smile.

***

Amber was studying in the library the next evening when she saw the Asian girl from her business class again. The girl was curled up in an oversize chair dozing a few feet away from her, an open book straddled across her lap. Amber noticed that the girl was so tiny, the chair looked as if it could envelop her sleeping form and devour her completely into its cushiony recesses. Amber pulled her gaze away from the girl and kept studying until from her peripheral vision she saw the girl awaken, yawn and stretch. The girl's movements were catlike and reminded her of the half-feral felines that roamed the farms back home in Wyoming. The girl looked around until she noticed Amber looking at her.

The girl offered a sheepish smile. "How long was I out?" she asked.

Amber shrugged. "I'm not really sure," she replied politely. Another student working nearby gave Amber and the girl a dirty look. The Asian girl glared back at the student in return.

"Chill out, we'll keep our voices down," she said. She stretched again as she stood up, her shirt rising ever so slightly. Amber caught a glimpse of the girl's cream-colored and very flat stomach. Quickly, she averted her eyes.

The girl walked over to Amber's table. "Hey, you're in my Biz One class. I saw you the other day." She extended her hand and decided to try out her American name on this girl. "I'm Lynn, spelled L-Y-N-N," she announced.

Amber hesitated before taking Lynn's hand. The assertiveness came as a surprise considering the fact that Lynn was so tiny and placid looking with the exception of her hair, which was styled like the punk rockers who her father swore were demons sent from hell.

"I'm Amber," she said.

Lynn laughed. "Yes you are. Just like your hair."

Amber touched her red locks self-consciously.

"It looks nice," Lynn said. "You're rocking that cut, girl."

"Oh!" Amber said, pleased. "Well, thanks."

"Anytime," Lynn said. They smiled at each other until Amber finally looked away. "Why are you sleeping in the library?" she asked with her Wyoming sensibleness. "Why not just go home and rest?"

Lynn's laugh sounded like a bark. "I live at home with my parents. They irk the hell out of me. Whenever I look at them, I think homicidal thoughts." She smiled slyly at Amber again. "Now with that being said, do you really want to send me home?"

Amber was startled by Lynn's frankness but she certainly understood where she was coming from. "No," she conceded somberly. "I guess you should just stay here for awhile."

Lynn laughed. She gave Amber an amused look. "You're a very grave and serious one," she said. "Where are you from?"

Amber paused just a second. "Midwest," she said vaguely. She had to be careful not to reveal too many personal details. In the back of her mind, she feared that her father might send spies to drag her kicking and screaming back home to Wyoming.

Lynn nodded, apparently satisfied with that answer. "I'm pretty much a native New Yorker," she said proudly. "Moved here with the fam when I was a young tot."

"Oh," Amber said. She paused. "So are you Chinese, Japanese…?" Her voice trailed off.

Lynn gave her an amused look. "Yeah, we Asians all look alike, I know. Not Chinese or Japanese. I'm Vietnamese."

"I'm so sorry," Amber apologized quickly as she felt her face flush, mortified at her own ignorance. There were no Asians in her hometown or in the surrounding areas of Brookville. Before coming to New York, the only people she had ever seen on a regular basis were white people.

Lynn shrugged. "Hey, it's okay. I'm just grateful you're not sending me home to kill my parents." Amber looked worried for a moment until she saw the playful grin on Lynn's face. "Oh, you should stop saying that," Amber chided but she was grinning too.

"So, do you live on or off campus, Miss Midwest?" Lynn asked, her dark eyes studying Amber intently. Amber didn't miss the intent gaze and felt her defenses rising.

"Why do you ask?" she said a little sharply.

Lynn recoiled in an exaggerated fashion. "Well, excuse me," she said. "Just asking, that's all. I can't afford to live in a dorm and the off-campus housing is too pricey for me. I might end up in a shelter or something, who knows?"

Amber relaxed a little. "It's okay, I overreacted. I live on campus in the Towers. My scholarship includes housing."

Lynn looked impressed. "Wow!" she said. "A full scholarship? You must be very smart."

Amber shrugged. She only knew how to be humble. "I do okay," she said quietly.

Lynn glanced at the time on her cell phone then stood up abruptly. "Well, I need to get going," she said. "I need to check out the shelters. Don't know which one I'll be staying at tonight but anywhere is better than going home."

Amber stared at Lynn. "You're really going to stay in a shelter tonight?" she asked incredulously. "Aren't those places…well…dangerous?"

Lynn cocked her head to the side. "Hey, I'm a tough New Yorker and don't you forget it," she said. Amber thought Lynn's smile looked forced, a little frightened.

Amber stood up too. "Why don't you stay with me tonight?" she offered. "You'll have to sleep on the couch but that's better than staying in a shelter. I have sheets and blankets you can use." Amber's conservative Wyoming upbringing wouldn't allow her to offer her roommate's bed without permission. She had been at City College for one month and had only seen her roommate about four times. Her roommate was a chatty buxom blonde from Philadelphia named Kim who spent most nights with her West African boyfriend in his dorm room.

Lyn looked relieved. "That'll be great. Thanks, Amber."

The walk to Amber's apartment was quiet except for the chirping sounds of crickets filling the night air. Amber was aware of Lynn's slight presence as she walked beside her, an earthy smell that reminded her of a musky incense radiating from her white skin with just a touch of olive in its color. They reached Amber's place and as Lynn stood behind her, Amber could almost feel Lynn's warm breath on her shoulder as she unlocked the door and turned on the lights.

"Wow!" Lynn exclaimed as she looked around the modestly furnished apartment. "Man, you are so lucky, you know?" She plopped down on a plaid couch and looked around with a big grin, her hands behind her head. "You have all this to yourself?"

Amber smiled as she sat in an overstuffed matching plaid chair. "I have a roommate but she's never around."

Lynn nodded slowly, still grinning. "Very cool," she said as she nodded slowly, perusing the place with her deep black eyes.

Amber stood up and gestured toward the couch where Lynn was sitting. "You can sleep there," she said. "I have an early class so I'm going to turn in, okay?"

Lynn gazed at her without saying anything, her lips curled into a tiny smile as if she had a secret.

Amber fidgeted before she looked away. "Well, goodnight," she said and then added hastily, "Do you need blankets and a pillow?"

Lynn laughed. "Don't need all that. It's still warm, you know."

Amber laughed too, not sure why she suddenly felt so nervous. "Well, sleep tight. Don't let the bedbugs bite."

Lynn gave her a sideways look. "Yeah, okay Midwest," she said as she stretched out on the couch and closed her eyes, ending the awkward banter. Amber stood there for a moment and when Lynn's eyes didn't open again, she mumbled goodnight one more time and hastily retreated to her bedroom.

Somewhere in the middle of the night Amber began to dream. There were footsteps in her dream, footsteps approaching her as she lay in bed too paralyzed to move. She tried to open her eyes but her eyelids were so heavy. She thought she should be afraid but she wasn't. The sleep was encasing her in a world that felt like fantasy; unreal and never ending. She dreamt that she felt something warm trailing her body from head to toe and then the warmth enveloped her in such a way that she had only read about, heard about from gossipy girls in her school back home. The warmth tickled her, teased her, brought her to a point to which she could only moan and writhe as she wished for the warmth never to stop. The warmth became more and more intense until she arched her back and screamed cries of ecstasy, of helplessness, the cries turning to deep emotional sobs only when she realized the warmth had dissipated.

The next morning when Amber awoke, Lynn was already awake. Amber felt small breasts pressed against her naked back as Lynn spooned against her and rubbed her back with deft, purposeful strokes.

"Well, good morning," Lynn said matter-of-factly. Amber couldn't speak for a few moments and when she did, her words were choppy, as if she was being strangled.

"Did you...did we...?"

Lynn stretched and grinned like a Cheshire cat, her naked body lean and smooth. "Yeah," she nodded her head with swagger. "We did. You were good, girl."

Amber stared into defiant almond-shaped eyes that refused to look away from hers.

"Oh my God," Amber finally groaned in disbelief as she buried her face in the pillow.

"Don't worry," Lynn sneered. "Your secret's safe with me." The knock on the door made Amber jump.

"Don't worry," Lynn said again as she bounded out of bed and quickly headed for the door. "I ordered breakfast from that place down the street."

Ordered breakfast? I thought you were broke, Amber thought, her numb mind still reeling from the shock of what Lynn claimed had happened between the two of them last night. As Amber was climbing out of bed, her knees buckled. Her legs felt like jelly and her feet were numb. She peered at herself in the mirror on her dresser. Her face was flushed and her scalp was soaked with sweat. As she clumsily began to comb her hair, she suddenly realized how good she felt. She was in New York and could finally assemble the pieces of her broken life. She had never liked dresses or anything feminine, including the long hair which thankfully was gone for good. Boys were low, if not nonexistent, on her radar. Under her father's rule of religious tyranny, she had never been free to understand her feelings until now. She now knew she was a lesbian and it was all right with her. She smiled, feeling lucky that she had met Lynn. They could have a relationship and offer emotional support to each other. They could build a life together and be happy. She was smiling as she put the comb down, then she heard Lynn speak in a guttural tone.

"Yeah man, she's in there like I promised. Where's my money, man?"

There was silence for a few seconds followed by a grumbled thanks, rapid footsteps, and the sound of the front door closing with finality.

Amber's brow furrowed in confusion. What? she asked herself and then she saw the Reverend John T. Owens filling the doorway of her bedroom with his massive girth. His ice blue eyes were empty yet fiery with his convictions. Margaret stared at him, frozen in her tracks like a deer in headlights.

"Get your things, Margaret. I'm taking you home."

Amber shook her head slowly at first as the reality of how Lynn had set her up sunk in, then faster and faster until she felt a searing pain shoot through her neck.

"No!" she screamed in horror, in sheer disbelief that her father had found her. She backed away from him. "Don't call me Margaret! My name is Amber!"

"Your name is sinner, fornicator, degenerate lover of women," he boomed as he slowly reached into his pocket and pulled out a hypodermic needle. He waved it menacingly in the air. "Submit and come with me quietly or I'll take you by force."

"Fuck you!" Amber screamed before he lunged at her and she felt the needle plunge deeply into the arm she had raised to shield herself. As Amber crumpled to the floor, everything faded to black.

***

When Margaret awakened, her mouth felt like cotton and her arm ached. She looked around, horrified. She wanted to scream but the cloth stuffed into her mouth prevented her from making a sound. She was in the woodshed in Brookville, seated and tied firmly to the base of a wooden post. Her right wrist was crossed and bound tightly over her left wrist, leaving only her hands and fingers free to move. She looked down. Her slacks were gone, replaced by one of the old fashioned gingham dresses she used to wear. She felt something heavy which streamed down her back. Someone had put a long red wig on her head which covered her short cropped locks. She peered up at the dark shadow looming over her.

"Welcome home, daughter," Reverend John T. Owens said.

Margaret watched through frightened eyes as her mother crept into the woodshed and timidly pushed a tray of food towards her. Her brother Joshua stood behind his mother holding a glass of water. He set it down beside his bound sister, his empty eyes staring straight through her.

"Margaret, how could you cut your hair?' her mother asked in a whisper. "A woman's hair is her crowning glory. You must repent. God will forgive you if you ask the Lord for forgiveness." Her mother and brother tiptoed out of the shed.

Margaret began to sob as she trembled in terror.

Reverend Owens gave her a long unemotional gaze. " I told my congregation you live in New York now, that you have left your family to dwell in homosexual shame with the big city sinners," he said. He started to leave, then turned and looked at his daughter, his eyes glistening with satisfaction.

"Your mother will bring you three square meals a day, breakfast, lunch, dinner. Your hands are free enough so you may eat and drink if you wish. No one will come looking for you, Margaret. You'll stay in this shed for the rest of your days on earth, until the Lord calls you home. If your mother and I precede you in going home to the Lord, I have directed Joshua to keep you under lock and key for your remaining years. If Joshua precedes you in going home to the Lord, you'll die in here but take comfort in the fact that you will join us in splendid glory to live with the Almighty Father but only if you repent. If you do not repent, you'll burn in hell for all eternity."

He turned on his heel and left his sobbing daughter tied in the woodshed with total darkness and a deafening silence as her lifelong companions.